# THE LOST GENERATION

## CONNOR WHITELEY

# DEDICATION

Thank you to all my readers without you I couldn't do what I love.

# CHAPTER 1

Empire Army Commander Blake Longbot had always loved travelling the Empire going world to world helping to reinforce the odd position, delivering supplies to planets that needed it most and just generally helping out the Empire and its wonderful citizens wherever he could. He certainly wasn't a battle-hardened Commander in the strictest of senses, because he wasn't that much of a fan of war per se.

It always sounded so strange to everyone else on his ship, The *Deliverance*, the Empire and the citizens that he spoke to most often. But it was the truth. And whilst the Great Human Empire was assaulted constantly by traitors, aliens and mutants, Blake was more than happy protecting the citizens away from the frontline.

Blake stood on his small semi-circular command bridge, which felt so amazing to be back on after its decoration (at the crew's insistence) and Blake had to admit it wasn't actually as bad as he feared.

The walls were perfectly smoothed and painted bright purple and violet and blues. It certainly wasn't his first colour choice but clearly the command crew, an all-female crew, had spoken amongst themselves and overruled him. And the perfect smoothness of the walls did look so much better than they used to with all the chipped, potted and shot-out dents in the walls.

Even the tiers upon tiers of blue holographic computers behind Blake looked great. The holograms looked so wonderfully crisp, sharp and the holograms didn't flash every so often as the computers were on their last legs. These computers were brilliant and new and so powerful that Blake was really looking forward to using them.

The delightful smells of pastries, strawberries and apricot jam filled the air and Blake seriously had to promote his best friend and first-mate Captain Charlotte for insisting that the bridge had its own food synthesiser that also created drinks. That was a great call and it really did show how amazing his command crew actually were.

It was even better that the wonderful taste of almond Danish pastries filled his tongue and it was so perfect with the background noise of his command crew laughing, swiping and banging away on their holographic keyboards.

Blake was pretty sure that the banging away sound was fake to add a little background noise to a bridge but Blake didn't care. He just liked to know his command crew was alive, well and happy behind him.

"Commander," Charlotte said as she came to stand next to him wearing her very tight blue Empire Navy uniform, her gun was at her waist and her sword was hanging down on the other side.

Blake was surprised that Charlotte looked perfect today of all days because all they were doing was travelling beyond Empire territory to reach an exploratory expedition that had sent out a distress call.

It wasn't exactly hard work so it really didn't require formal dress in the slightest. Blake was only wearing his green Empire Army uniform because he hadn't done any washing lately and he hadn't given the task to someone under his command.

"We should be with the fleet within three hours," Charlotte said.

Blake smiled. That would give him plenty of time to talk with his wonderful command crew and see whatever gadgets they installed on the bridge during the decoration that he didn't know about.

But for now, Blake simply stared out of the immense diamond-shaped floor-to-ceiling windows that seemed so perfect now with its crystal-clear glass, freshly painted black framing and the holograms embedded into the windows seemed so much sharper than the last ones. The old holograms made Blake feel like he was going blind at times.

At least everything was looking up for them now

and in a few centuries Blake would be able to retire, but that scared him a lot. Blake couldn't imagine retiring from the Empire Army and helping people so he was only slightly glad that was centuries away.

"Um Commander," Charlotte said, and Blake realised she was looking at a black dataslate in her hand.

"What?" Blake asked. He had no idea whatsoever why she would be concerned, there were no reports of aliens, traitors or mutants in the area and there weren't even any planets coming up on their path.

"I have a ship reading on our screens from two solar systems over and, I don't know, our sensors can't identify it," Charlotte said.

Blake shrugged. "Run a more detailed scan please and adjust course slightly so we can get close to it,"

The entire ship hummed slightly and Blake was rather excited about this ship. It was so rare to find a ship out in this no-man's-lands of space so it would just be amazing to discover something.

"That cannot be right," Charlotte said walking back over to Blake after talking to the command crew. "Commander you have to see this,"

Blake clapped his hands and turned around so it activated the blue holograms in the centre of the bridge, revealing an in-depth scan of a solar system with ten planets, a small sun and a very large ship floating there.

From the holograms it was hard to make out the true size and shape of the ship but it looked to be oval with spires rising out of the surface. And it appeared to be human made.

"Commander there is no easy way to say this but that ship is human," Charlotte said.

Blake had to admit that wasn't news so he pressed a finger against the cold hologram and streams of data appeared in front of him but only one piece of information caught his eye.

The scans were telling him this ship wasn't Empire, it wasn't Old Earth and it wasn't transmitting any signals they could interact with.

"Scan the transmitting signals through the databases. Maybe the databases can identify it," Blake said.

This was just flat out strange. As far as he knew the cultures of Old Earth never got past their own solar system or maybe a few solar systems outside Sol but then humanity had collapsed and been enslaved by the techno-barbarians up until a hundred thousand years ago when the Emperor reunited humanity.

"Damn it," Charlotte and all the other command crew said as one.

Blake scanned the data streams in front of him and it was amazing.

"This ship is transmitting signals we haven't seen in three hundred thousand years," Blake said completely amazed. "This would make it older than the Empire, older than the techno-barbarians and this would make that ship Old Earth technology,"

"Correction," a tall woman wearing a red

uniform said. "This is actually the only Generation Ship Old Earth ever sent off into space,"

Blake gasped and the entire crews' mouth dropped. Everyone in the Empire had heard about the concept of generation ships and how amazing they were but everyone believed it was just a fantasy from Old Earth.

But one existed. And Blake had no idea what to do except from call in the experts.

"Highest level encryption Charlotte. Contact Empire Regional Space Alpha Priority. Tell them we need historical experts immediately," Blake said.

"Of course commander,"

Blake knew it would easily take three months for the nearest Empire Research Fleet to arrive at the ship so Blake fully intended to help the exploratory fleet then circle back around and start scanning that Generation Ship.

The least he could do whilst the Research Fleet arrived was simply try to give them as much data as possible.

And this seriously excited Blake a lot more than he ever wanted to admit.

# CHAPTER 2

Chief Historical Expert Nathan Lordy was so, so excited about today because his ship, *The Curious*, would finally break out of Slidespace after four long months and he would be able to see the so-called Generation Ship at long, long last.

Nathan couldn't believe how amazing of an opportunity this was to research such an incredible piece of Old Earth technology. And well, if this truly was a Generation Ship then by now there would be billions of people on board so Nathan could research them, study them and see what Old Earth was actually like.

He would be famous, he would be invited to give speeches and he would be one of the richest people in the Empire.

Of course Nathan never did anything for the money and to be honest most of the time Nathan just donated all of his salary to various charities all over the Empire because he hardly needed it. His work, travelling the Empire and researching was his life and money wasn't needed too much.

Nathan stood right in front of some small waist-height windows on his square bridge with his breath fogging up the windows he was standing so close to it. He just wanted the slidespace jump to be over so he could see this beautiful piece of technology.

Nathan had never spent too much time on the bridge because he loved his library, kitchen and lab too much to waste his time on actually managing the ship. He had always left that to his wonderful brother, Patrick, and his wife, Ruby.

Both of them were gifted historians in their own right and Nathan really loved having them on board, because each of them had expertise in different areas and they all combined their knowledge to become a powerful team. Nathan wasn't sure if they were that powerful because Nathan just loved his family, but all the journals, books and reports highlighting how great they were said it.

The bridge itself wasn't as grand as those of warships and Nathan liked that. He hated going to explore wrecked Empire Army ships from thousands of years ago because they were so big, spacious and they were all holograms.

That made them next to useless from a historical perspective. Especially when the stick that Nathan used to download the ship's content wasn't downloadable. When that happened it was just a massive pain in the ass.

"Slidespace jump ends in ten minutes bro," Patrick said.

Nathan forced himself to look away from the windows and he smiled at his brother. He really was looking smart today which wasn't like him at all, he couldn't remember the last time his brother had worn a shirt, trousers and black shoes.

Nathan wondered if he had missed a birthday, anniversary or something else entirely, but he hadn't, this time. And when Ruby walked in wearing a long black dress Nathan really felt underdressed in his white lab coat with his father's thin battle armour underneath.

He wasn't exactly sure why he always wore the battle armour, it had been useless on wreckage exploration and exploring historical sites in bad warzones but besides from that, he supposed it was just comfortable.

"I've signalled the warship we'll be entering the system momentarily and the Commander has given us three permission to teleport aboard," Ruby said.

Nathan bit his lip. He wasn't a fan of talking to military people because they were often harsh, dismissive and thought of Nathan's work as a complete and utter waste of time, but most of the Empire's most revolutionary inventions could trace their roots back to a historical piece of Old Earth tech.

"And the Commander's gay," Ruby said.

Nathan shook his head as soon as he realised

exactly what Ruby and Patrick were saying, and that was why they had dressed up. They wanted to show the Commander that they were respectful, wonderful people and that Nathan was a catch.

"Before you protest bro just admit you need to get a boyfriend for mum's new wedding," Patrick said.

Nathan just smiled because that was sadly true. Their mother was thankfully remarrying after his father died to a great man and Nathan really couldn't go to a wedding single.

"I'm fine about it," Nathan said.

"Good bro," Patrick said.

Nathan grabbed a dataslate and projected a hologram of the Generation Ship into the bridge. It was a very large oval shape with a domed-bottom that presumably contained all the engines and other pieces of technology and then there were spires and skyscrapers coming out of the top.

Nathan was more than grateful for the early data but until he was actually in the system and could use his own equipment, he just couldn't know anything for sure.

"Slidespace jumps ends… now," Ruby said.

Nathan spun around and his mouth dropped as they entered the system. He had never seen such a beautiful stunning ship in all his life.

The Generation Ship was simply a work of art with its dusty dull metal bottom that was perfectly domed like a bowl. Three hundred kilometres above the dome was nothing but perfectly straight sides of the ship so probably that was probably were the apartments, factories and farms were.

Then the golden spires were simply stunning as they sparkled like angelic diamonds against the rest of the ship as the small sun shone back.

"Scan it now," Nathan said.

"But the Commander wants to meet us," Ruby said.

"Scan it. Please," Nathan said feeling so excited.

Nathan heard his brother and sister-in-law start a scan but they both walked back over a few moments later.

"Bro there should be people on this ship right?"

Nathan laughed. "Of course. I estimate by this point in history there should easily be billions onboard,"

"Then why can I find no life signs and no bodies onboard?"

Nathan just grinned. That was a hell of a puzzle and one that Nathan seriously wanted to find out more about. What the hell happened to all those people?

# CHAPTER 3

As the cold darkness of the solar system flashed blue for a moment as the Research ship, *The Curious*, rematerialised and exited Slidespace, Blake had to admit that he was so, so excited to meet the amazing researchers on the ship. When he requested Empire support four months ago, he had been livid with Empire Command for saying the mission wasn't urgent and that was what caused the month's delay.

But now that the amazing and legendary researchers were here, Blake just couldn't believe how excited he felt. Ever since they had learnt who was coming to help them the entire ship had been buzzing.

Behind Blake the command crew were all jumping up and down, talking and their voices were filled with excitement. Blake couldn't blame them for a single second, Dr Patrick, Nathan and Ruby Lordy were such legends in the historical worlds of the Empire that it was impossible not to know them.

Of course Blake had no idea who they were until exactly until now, but he had read all the papers, books and seminar reports in the past four months and they were just amazing.

Blake had gone to university and he even held a doctorate in Early Empire Studies but he had never used it. And when he had been at university, he actually had no idea an author could write this riveting about events of the past.

It was mind-blowing.

"Double checking permission to teleport," Charlotte said more of a statement rather than a question and she too was failing to hide her excitement.

Blake nodded so much he thought he was about to hurt his neck.

But as the wonderful temperature of the bridge rose, the breathtaking smells of apricot jam, pastries and strawberries filled the air, Blake just knew that this was the perfect welcome for such delightful people onto the bridge.

"Permission granted again," Blake said.

"Teleporting now," Charlotte said.

Blake waved the members of the command crew back behind their tiers of holographic computers and Blake pressed his back against the icy cold metal windows as blue smoke swirled, whirled and twirled in the centre of the bridge.

Then three people appeared.

Blake's mouth dropped when he saw a very

beautiful Ruby Lordy standing there in a long black dress that showed off how beautiful she was.

But his focus really went to Patrick Lordy who looked gorgeous in his white shirt, black trousers and shoes. He looked like such a beautiful gentleman so it was just a shame he was straight and Ruby was his wife.

"Hello Commander it is such an honour to be here," a shorter man said as he came towards Blake.

Blake's mouth just dropped even more, turned dry and his brain turned to mush as he stared at the utterly stunning man in his little white lab coat and thin battle armour showing underneath. He was so stunningly perfect with his brown hair, handsome face and massive smile that Blake was lost for words.

"Wow," Blake said.

"Wow what?" the cutie asked smiling.

Blake immediately wanted to say that he was wow but he couldn't. He needed to least pretend to be a little professional.

"It is rare that I get to meet such legends in the historical worlds," Blake said.

All three of the historians laughed.

Cute Nathan grinned at Blake. "And you are fairly legendary too Commander Blake, your doctorate thesis on Events of the Unification War shaped the way most citizens think about the formation of the Empire and its early years. It was a revolutionary paper,"

Blake was just shocked. He had no idea that his

doctorate thesis had been published but that would explain the few thousand credits he got in his bank account every month like clockwork. He had no idea who published it (most probably the university) but clearly it was selling like crazy.

"Thank you," Blake said. "It was only a passionate project and I am excited to get into this Generation Ship,"

"Oh, so are we," Nathan said, and Blake had to admit that it was so wonderful to see how excited, happy and cheerful this beautiful man was.

Blake knew that he was going to seriously love working with this amazing team.

"This is Captain Charlotte," Blake said gesturing to his best friend. "This is the best command crew I have ever worked with and per protocol, our resources are yours, and your resources are ours,"

"Brilliant," Ruby said as she went over to the tiers upon tiers of holographic computers and started shaking the hands of a very quiet command crew. This was the quietest Blake had ever seen them.

"Commander, have you conducted a full scan of the Generation Ship yet?" Nathan asked.

Blake forced his mouth to work as the two of them went over to the middle of the bridge. "Yes and that's where things get very weird,"

Blake clapped his hands and a blue hologram appeared showing an immense city with millions of apartments, systems and complex buildings that Blake rarely saw in Empire space stations let alone Old

Earth tech.

Nathan stared at the hologram like this was magical. And Blake had to admit that it was in a way because it would take a good week or two for them to understand the layout of the Generation Ship and understand the sheer scale of it, but there was a more pressing matter to Blake.

"*Deliverance*," Blake said to the ship. "Going on Old Earth data, how large should the population be after three hundred thousand years?"

"Ten billion at the most," the ship said in a very computerised voice that thankfully wasn't as high-pitched as the last one before the decoration.

"On the hologram show us in red dots the location of the bodies or living people," Blake said.

"Cannot. There are no data points for such a request," the *Deliverance* said.

The entire command crew gasped and Blake just looked at Nathan. It made no sense whatsoever why there were no bodies or living people on that Generation ship after so long.

And Blake had absolutely no idea why and that seriously scared him but also excited him a little.

He loved a good mystery and that was a massive one.

# CHAPTER 4

As much as Nathan just wanted to explore the absolutely stunning Generation Ship a few kilometres from them, he sadly had to force himself to follow protocol in the strictest sense for the next week, but he had to admit that he had loved every single moment on the breathtaking bridge standing out like a sore thumb because of his white lab coat and thin battle armour underneath

The bridge might have been semi-circular, have massive windows and have strange tiers of holographic computers but Nathan really enjoyed it. The command crew were always a laugh, some of them pranked each other and it was always such a fun atmosphere here.

Thankfully Patrick and Ruby had left the *Deliverance* and they were currently running scans, researching and cooking up a storm back on *The Curious*. Nathan made a point to talk to them at least three times a day so everyone was on the same page of the research, and the sheer amount was stunning.

Nathan had researched massive structures before from Old Earth and the odd Old Earth colony world that had been discovered, but this Generation Ship was simply something else.

Their scans had showed evidence of billions of people living on the Ship at some point or another. All the millions of small but very expensive-looking (at least by modern standards) apartments were filled, every level of the Ship had evidence of use and the green spaces were still active.

Nathan had no idea why so many billions of people simply vanished. Especially when the ship did had enough power to transmit the locator beacon, keep its shields intact so small dust particles wouldn't put a hole in the ship and the green spaces on the ship were thriving.

But there also had to be another functioning system that maintained the gardens so the entire ship didn't become one overgrown forest.

There were simply so many data points, questions and ideas floating between the crews of the *Deliverance* and Curious that Nathan had no idea where to begin, but at least that meant he got to spend a little more amazing time with Commander Blake.

Nathan still couldn't believe how stunning the man was. He had always been drawn to men actually but never ever as strongly as he was to Blake. There was just something so charming, warming and wonderful about him.

Not only was Blake caring but there was such a wisdom to him and his words and his historical perspective that it was so refreshing to encounter someone intelligent that wasn't his brother or sister-in-law.

"Chai latte?" Blake asked as he held two piping hot mugs of heavily spiced goodness in his hands.

"Thank you," Nathan said taking the wonderfully warm mug and the hints of cinnamon, coffee and sugar filled his senses.

"The command crew have found a possible hangar we can fly into when the time comes," Blake said.

Nathan frowned a little. It wasn't that he was against flying into a location but it almost seemed wrong to trespass on such a time capsule of human history with something as loud, noisy and disrupting as one of the Empire's blade-like shuttles.

"I agree," Blake said smiling. "Let's teleport in. It's more controlled, it couldn't strain the Ship as much as a shuttle is a lot heavier than we are and hopefully we can send a probe in sooner or later,"

Nathan was really liking how Blake thought, but he was right though. The sooner they sent a probe in the better, at least they would start to understand what atmosphere they were dealing with.

"I'll get my brother to set up a probe and launch it later on. I would like to rule out air-born toxins before we board,"

Blake laughed. "That would be nice because the

position of the ship is annoying me,"

Nathan grinned and he started pacing around the bridge. He had had the exact same thought a few days ago but dismissed it. He was so glad he wasn't being silly.

"*Deliverance*," Nathan said. "Bring up an image of Milky Way Galaxy at the time of the launch,"

A few seconds later the ship hummed loudly and a dull blue hologram appeared showing the Sol System in the middle and all the other tens of thousands of solar systems around it.

"We know from historical documents and the Emperor's personal knowledge," Nathan said, "that the Generation Ship headed north but that's the problem,"

"We're in the South of the galaxy and we're extreme south," Blake said. "How the hell did the Generation Ship get so off course?"

"And why didn't the Generation Ship crew abort the mission, return to Earth and fix their navigation equipment if it was that faulty? They would have travelled straight past Earth to come south,"

Nathan shrugged to his own question. He was really hoping that exploring the navigation equipment of the ship would give them some kind of answers but the command crew had been trying to hack their way into the ship for days.

It was impossible because modern and ancient systems just didn't want to work together.

"We need to get on that Generation Ship,"

Nathan said. "Do you think you know the layout well enough?"

Nathan nodded. It wouldn't be hard to render their scans into a holographic map that they could use when they were aboard but it was the atmosphere that was really concerning Nathan.

He just couldn't understand what had caused so many people to disappear so there was a good chance it was an environmental problem. And the very last thing Nathan wanted to do was take his brother, sister-in-law and sexy Blake into a Ship that would literally kill them.

Nathan had to get that probe launched now.

# THE LOST GENERATION

# CHAPTER 5

Blake absolutely couldn't understand the results two days later whatsoever as he, sexy Nathan and his brother Patrick stood on the bridge of *The Curious* looking at the final results of the probe they had sent in.

Blake had to admit he wasn't the biggest fan of the square bridge of *The Curious* because it was just so small, it smelt of burnt ozone and oil and it simply wasn't as nice as the *Deliverance* but it meant he got to spend even more time with Nathan so that was simply perfect to him.

As the very last of the data from the probe appeared in front of them, Blake just couldn't believe what he was reading. The probe had a perfectly functioning environmental system throughout the entire Generation Ship. That had to be simply impossible.

Whenever Blake had done research in the past about history, he had always been able to find some little factor that started the chain of events that led to a civilisation falling. Old Earth's downfall had started when they gave full independence to the various colony planets that meant when those planets allied themselves against Old Earth, Old Earth got shut out of trade, military and all sorts of deals.

Old Earth didn't have much of a water supply, a farming industry or anything after its stupid wars so it depended on those colony planets to send in supplies. And so Old Earth dissolved into tribes and eventually the Techno-barbarians took over until the Coming Of The Emperor.

There was nothing like that here.

Blake couldn't identify a single factor so far that lead to this disappearance.

"Take a closer look at the exact proportion of chemical elements and compounds in the air please," Nathan said.

"Sure thing bro,"

Blake was stunned as well. This simply couldn't be happening and it did raise a lot of exciting questions, but right now Blake was rather enjoying looking at the beautiful man next to him.

Nathan was still wearing his strange white lab coat and Blake seriously didn't understand why Nathan wore thin battle armour under it, he wasn't a soldier but it did make him look hot though.

"I'll contact the *Deliverance* and get them to start preparing for a boarding mission. We'll wear full enviro-suits just in case," Blake said.

"Good," Nathan said. "I would like to say this was going to be easy but it is rather fascinating. And those secrets will be on that ship,"

Blake was about to agree when he realised that this wasn't just a boarding mission for a few hours or until the fight was over. This was an investigative mission so they were going to need miniature food synthesisers and a number of items to enable them to stay on the Ship for longer periods of time.

Blake clicked his fingers and bright blue holograms appeared in front of him so he called Charlotte.

"Captain I need you to get us some enviro-suits sorted and enough equipment for an Investigative Mission. Are you familiar with the protocols?"

It was a stupid question because the protocol exams were probably the only ones Charlotte aced but Blake wanted to be professional at the very least.

"Of course Commander and last night I just finished reading the new Official Guidelines. They were fascinating. I'll get the equipment straight away,"

Blake cut the line before he said something a little harsh about how sad it was that Charlotte got excited about some mere guidelines. Blake hadn't read them for years and he was the Commander.

Nathan stepped closer and Blake enjoyed the feeling of his body against his until he realised that Nathan was pointing towards the top of one of the spires.

Blake frowned when he noticed that it was

glowing bright gold.

Blake clicked his fingers again and started to run a scan of the spire only to realise that it was scanning them in return.

"Nothing," Blake said. "There isn't a person on board or anything. The Ship itself is deciding to scan us,"

Nathan gasped and grinned like a little kid. Blake was so glad he was with him because this was so strange but so amazing. The very idea that a mere empty ship could decide for itself to scan something was revolutionary. It was a stunning idea.

"So we know that the ship has billions of people missing, an environment perfect to support life and has the ability to scan whenever it feels the need. That is a little strange," Blake said.

"Yea mate," Patrick said as he came back over. "We have another problem. The reports of elements and compounds in the air is identical to samples of Old Earth in something called the $21^{st}$ Century whatever that is. The air is fine and identical to what it should be to support life,"

Blake just laughed. There was no clear reason why the ship couldn't possibly support life or what on Earth it had done with all the bodies.

"Any pathogens or bacteria?" Nathan asked. Blake realised it was a good question before he already knew the answer.

"None whatsoever. There were some fungi and harmless bacteria found in the air but nothing more than in the air of our ships mate,"

Blake rolled his eyes. It was a shame that humans could never survive in a bacteria-free environment but at least they knew that there wasn't a disease that wiped out the population either.

Nathan just looked at Blake. "I need access to the Generation Ship. Now,"

And as much as Blake didn't want to go inside just yet, he knew they had no other choice whatsoever. The secrets to this mystery was inside that ship.

A ship that had been locked away and undiscovered for three hundred thousand years and that number was impossible for Blake to wrap his head around.

But it was extremely exciting and Blake really wanted to get onboard.

## CHAPTER 6

Nathan was so, so glad that *The Curious* didn't have immense grey metal hangars with oddly perfectly smooth walls, a horrible smell of burnt oil and rubber and with so many crew members running in and out the noise was simply deafening off the smooth walls.

Normally before a mission and one as potentially dangerous as this one, Nathan liked to prepare in a quiet hangar or the bridge itself, and not some busy hangar with blade-like fighters and shuttles and transports hanging off the ceiling like bats. Clearly the crew of The *Deliverance* didn't feel the same way.

Nathan stood with beautiful Blake, Ruby and Patrick as all of them finished getting on their bright yellow environmental suits that were styled on the superhuman Angel armour that in itself was styled on the armour of medieval knights of Old Earth. The armour was a little thinner but that was perfect for Nathan because his father's armour and lab armour made up for it.

Nathan knelt down and picked up his small black rucksack that contained his scanners, equipment and even some test tubes in case there was something he wanted to sample and bring back to conduct further tests on.

"We know where we're going right?" Ruby asked. "The ship should teleport us four to the lower deck near the old Education Centre,"

Nathan felt his stomach fill with butterflies. He was so excited about this. This was going to be such an amazing trip with even more amazing people and it meant he got to spend some more wonderful time with sexy Blake.

"Launch us when you're ready," Nathan said to Blake.

Nathan was so glad to see Blake grinning through his helmet and he pressed a button signaling to the bridge that they were ready to be teleported. Nathan took a deep breath of the freshly recycled air of the suit and grinned as the teleportation started to happen.

Tendrils of bright blue smoke swirled, whirled and twirled around them and the ground simply fell away from Nathan.

Nathan's body shook hard. Something was wrong. The smoke turned blood red.

Nathan smashed into something. His suit ripped. Something sliced into his arm.

He smashed into something else.

Then again and again.

The smoke faded and Nathan pounded the ground he landed firmly on his ass.

Nathan gasped and took his deep breaths of the refreshing damp air and he actually had no idea what had happened let alone where he actually was. His heart pounded in his chest.

Nathan forced himself to calm down and he just managed to make his mind focus enough to him to see that in amongst the pitch darkness of wherever he was, the dim light coming off his helmet revealed he was in something metal.

That was a good sign actually because it meant that he was on the Generation Ship and he hadn't rematerialised in the icy cold void of space. That would have been an instant death sentence if he had.

But Nathan couldn't understand what on earth had actually caused the teleportation malfunction. The one that had just happened to him was a lot worse than the average mishap.

Teleportation wasn't perfect perfect but it was still good to almost never go wrong. And it sure as hell never went wrong quite like that, and Nathan bit his lip as he realised the Generation Ship must have done that.

He had no idea how the Generation Ship could interfere with technology that wasn't available back in the time of Old Earth but he just knew that it had. And Nathan had no idea what had happened to the others.

Nathan slowly forced himself up and held out his

hands in front of his face and it was damn well annoying that he couldn't see them. Perhaps when he smashed into something and his suit tore it had damaged some of the wires connected to the headtorch.

It wasn't ideal but Nathan simply went to take off his rucksack and cursed when he didn't feel it attached to him. His damn rucksack had been atomised probably, he no longer had a spare torch.

Nathan took a few steps forward and felt warm metal that the more he touched the more he realised it was a wall of some kind.

A strange sound that could have been a language echoed overhead but Nathan had no idea what it was saying. It sounded so primitive compared to the Empire tongue that Nathan really wasn't sure if it was words or not.

"Come in bro," Patrick said over the suit's communicator. Nathan was so glad his brother was alive.

"I'm alive. Where are you? Do you have lights?"

"Negative bro. Me and Ruby are together. I cannot get Blake up on the communicators. What the hell happened?"

Nathan just froze as he heard the Generation Ship hum to alive and slowly bright white lights flickered on.

Revealing a sterile white corridor in the shape of a tube was what Nathan was standing in and there wasn't a speckle of dust or dirt or blood on the walls.

It was perfectly intact like it was brand-new from the factory.

It sort of made sense for the lights to turn on as a reaction to movement as it would have helped the crew and population to save energy. But why was it activating now after so long?

"No idea but be careful. No risks and report on movements every ten minutes. Do you understand," Nathan said.

"Yeah bro. Stay safe. The Emperor Protects,"

Nathan just smiled as Patrick cut the line because as much as he loved that Empire Army saying he actually had no idea how the hell the Emperor could protect them in a Generation Ship that clearly wasn't normal at all.

And Nathan had to force his heart to stop pounding in his chest when he realised that beautiful Blake could be dead.

## CHAPTER 7

Blake hated the sheer pain that flooded down his arm when he woke up, he had no idea whatsoever how long he had been knocked out for but that had to be the worse teleportation he had ever had. And Blake had had a hell of a lot of them over the decades.

Thankfully it was basic training to be even more careful after a teleportation mishap but Blake had to admit that now the lights were on in the Generation Ship he was just a little creeped out.

Blake was sitting in some of garden-like building with immense crystal clear tubes of water hanging all over the ceiling and walls transporting thousands of litres of water per second. It was so incredible to see it still functioning after all this time, and the constant sound of running water, filter pumping it about and the splashing of water into some kind of planet pot in the centre of the room was simply amazing.

Blake liked how the bright white lights reflected

perfectly off the flowing water so it created a rainbow effect that danced wonderful lights and colours onto the bright white walls of the garden area.

Blake was even more impressed that he was stuck in-between rows upon rows of white plastic trenches, not filled with any soil but from the look of them they were filled with dead plants and flowing water.

Maybe that was why the billions of people had disappeared. Maybe it was water related. Maybe he had finally solved it.

Blake huffed as the only problem with that theory was that the air was perfectly okay and the probe would have tested water if it found anything. That was just so damn annoying and Blake hated that he was no closer to finding out what had happened to the billions on the ship.

Blake carefully looked around his surroundings and was more than glad to see the teleportation hadn't made a part of him rematerialise inside something solid. The last thing he wanted was to have a finger or arm embedded in the floor.

Blake slowly stood up in case one of his body parts was trapped somewhere and he hadn't realised it. Thankfully he had been right the first time and the sheer scale of this garden area was simply stunning. It easily stretched for tens upon tens of kilometres so at least he now knew how the people on the ship were fed. They literally grew all their own food in these hydronic gardens.

A minor pain pulsed down his right shoulder and

thankfully the pain was nowhere near as bad as it once was which was great. Blake wasn't a fan of teleportation mishaps let alone when the silly mishap made him smash into something.

Blake had probably smashed into one of the plastic trenches where he rematerialised but at least he hadn't broken anything. That was a very common occurrence and Blake wasn't liking the idea that he was only still alive through luck.

He really, really hoped that Patrick, Ruby and wonderful Nathan, the man he was falling for, was okay.

Blake went to start walking towards a large circular door that he noticed in the distance but he looked up and his mouth dropped even more. The hydroponic gardens stretched upwards for a good ten kilometres too and there were even more dead plants and floating trenches in the ceiling.

It was simply mind-bending that there was enough space here and trenches to grow food in to feed billions of people very well. It was amazing and Blake actually didn't know a single place in the Empire that could compare to this wonderful marvel.

Equally the Empire had entire worlds dedicated to food production, smaller scale hydroponic gardens and food synthesisers so maybe the Empire hadn't fallen behind Old Earth. But this garden was still stunning.

Blake went down the long, long row of trenches he had been teleported into and the sound of cracking filled the air so Blake kept moving and he looked down. The black plastic and metal casing of his communicator was being smashed under his boot.

Blake had no idea how the damn communicator that was in his pocket had gotten attached to his boot but it had now. And now it was destroyed. Blake just hated teleportation mishaps.

Yet as the white plastic trenches started moving into the air and they kept rotating around in an immense circle, Blake had a feeling that this Generation Ship seriously wasn't as dead as they believed and now Blake really wanted to know exactly where beautiful Nathan, Patrick and Ruby were.

Something dangerous was clearly going on. The Generation Ship itself had to be behind the teleportation mishap, something that should have been impossible because teleportation didn't exist in the Old Earth cultures, but somehow this ship was trying to kill them.

Of that Blake had little doubt.

## CHAPTER 8

As soon as Nathan found another person or a reflective surface or just something, he was absolutely going to have to check his back because he had no idea what the teleportation had done to it but his back was hurting. Seriously hurting. Nathan was glad that he was wearing his white lab coat and thin battle armour under his enviro-suit so at least he knew his back wasn't cut or anything.

There had been a minor cut on his arm earlier but thankfully the enviro-suit had sealed the wound or something. Nathan didn't know how it worked but he was just glad it did.

And now Nathan just couldn't shake the feeling that he was being watched intensely.

Nathan popped up a little white circular door and went into a very long tube-shaped chamber that flared to life instantly.

The tube chamber had a great smell of lavenders, oranges and clementines that filled the air almost like they were trying to cover up something else. The wonderful smell left the taste of orange tarts on his tongue just like how he used to make them with his mother when he was a kid and Patrick would come to steal them when they were still piping hot. Silly boy.

Nathan really did love his brother but he just couldn't afford to think about that right now, he had to focus and it would only be a few minutes until Patrick and Ruby contacted him again with their ten-minute update.

The chamber started to hum a little before falling silent and Nathan went into the chamber and it was interesting that there were really large pods that looked like white hot tubs that Nathan had seen in various luxury holo-brochures of hotels.

Nathan had no idea why the people on the Generation Ship would ever need to have a hot tub, so why they would have so many in one place. Surely the whole idea was to have a hot tub in a private location so not every Tom, Dick and Harry could see their naked parts.

Of course Patrick and Ruby only went to naked ones and Nathan didn't go at all. He couldn't think of anything worse than a hot tub, he didn't even like baths, they were such a waste of time and resources. He just stuck with showers.

Nathan went over to one of the hot tubs, found a small clip that presumably opened it and he pulled it open.

Nathan was shocked when the smell of acid, rot

and cooked meat filled the air as he realised what had once been in the crystal-clear water of the hot tub. This wasn't a hot tub, it was somewhere that the Generation Ship put bodies.

As much as Nathan really wished he had his black rucksack at the moment so he could test the water. He was fairly sure he would find high levels of calcium from human bones but there might not have been any visible bones or flesh in the water, but there didn't have to be.

The hot tub was probably air-tight so the air containing the smell of the dead bodies would be trapped for thousands of years until he opened it.

Nathan just couldn't believe why on earth these people of the Generation Ship would dissolve their bodies like this but then he noticed just how many hot tubs there were. There had to be easily a hundred or more here so there were a lot of bodies to dissolve, and Nathan was surprised at how many pipes and cables were connected to the tubs.

So maybe the hot tubs dissolved the bodies into the water to help feed a garden or something.

Nathan had to admit it was a hell of a thing to see and it was even more amazing that the tubs still seemed to work after all these thousands of years. And that was the one question that Nathan flat out couldn't understand. What the hell had happened to all the humans on the ship if everything still worked?

It made no sense but Nathan closed the hot tub and kept on walking down the long tube chamber. At least he understood how the Generation Ship fertilised its crops and that was an academic paper in itself but Nathan just knew there were a lot more secrets to discover before their mission was done.

And Nathan felt his stomach twist into a painful knot when he realised it had been four minutes since Ruby and Patrick had meant to call him.

Nathan had to find them as soon as possible.

# CHAPTER 9

Blake was so relieved to finally get out of that damn hydroponic garden, he wasn't against it in the slightest but it was just so big that it took him running at full speed half an hour to reach the door that allowed him to escape. If there was ever a mission to live on the Generation Ship there was no way in hell that Blake was ever going to sign up for it.

Blake had been walking about the long white corridor of the ship for ages now and Blake went into another chamber. Strange noises or groans filled the air which might have been a language but even though Blake had a doctorate in Early Empire Studies and sometimes work made him investigate the primitive languages of Old Earth he had no idea what this noise was. It really could have been just a sound for all he knew.

When the bright white lights slowly flicked on, Blake was amazed at the sight of hundreds of thousands of little white pods that were stacked up perfectly straight in massive stacks with there being a hole in the ceiling where the stacks ended.

Blake had actually read academic papers addressing these sort of ruins before. It turned out back on Old Earth they didn't have shuttles, warships and teleportation to get them around so they built strange little "cars" that eventually self-drove. Blake had read tons of papers on the silly notion of "cars" because they were expensive, non-efficient and compared to modern Empire technology they were so impractical.

There had been a handful of projects of the past few thousand years to give Empire people the experience of a car but they were so much hard work to drive, and they always failed. And as much as Blake loved history he was never going to get in a "car" they were death sentences. Equally he was sure that if the Empire ever fell and new version of humanity took over they would think the same about their tech.

That just made Blake smile. He really did love history and the future.

More and more of the strange noises that might have been a language filled the air and even the language was a little strange. Clearly the Generation Ship had a language that wasn't in any Empire database, which was fairly complete because the Emperor who had apparently lived through Old Earth had added all the known languages and Blake had studied those records.

He had never heard of this at all.

Blake went deeper into the chamber and he was surprised when a large white pod hummed off the top of a stack and slowly started to flow down towards him. This Generation Ship was remarkable considering that billions of people were missing and everything still seemed to be working fine.

After a few moments, the pod stopped in front of him and part of it dissolved allowing Blake to get inside.

He really didn't want to but if anything on the Generation Ship still worked then maybe this was the key to him finding beautiful Nathan and the others. It was a crazy idea but Blake was out of options.

It was flat out impossible to explore the entire Generation Ship and somehow find the others at the same time.

Blake stepped into the pod and coughed at the musty smell of it. The pod clearly didn't have enviro-systems and then two pink holograms appeared in front of him in a language Blake didn't understand.

He recognised the symbols in the holograms were probably words for something but he didn't know what they were.

"Take me to the other humans," Blake said to the pod doubting it was going to work.

"Translating and updating modern dictionary," a computerised voice said. "Machine Learning Programmes indicate human speech is very advance now. We will need more data to initiate a full learning sequence and full translation of Chinese to Modern

Dialect,"

Blake was stunned but in all fairness it was nothing that the Empire didn't use to some extent. They had machines and programmes that took the basic assumption that all human colonies and Empire worlds evolved using the same language first and then over time different dialects and sub-languages formed. And clearly the Emperor had known tons of languages back in the time of the Old Earth and when he reunited humanity everyone spoke like him or tried to.

Hence the creation of a base language for the Empire and somehow this Generation Ship technology was so advanced that it had worked out how to translate old languages to modern Empire tongue.

Fascinating.

"Three humans identified. Two together. One alone. Do you wish them to be teleported aboard?" the computer asked.

Blake shook his head. That was the last thing he wanted. This Generation Ship didn't want teleportation to happen and it had already tried to kill them all once so Blake was hardly going to give them another chance.

"Pick them up please, and can you give me an estimate journey time please?" Blake asked.

"Of course," the computer said. "It will take us two hours to reach the couple. They are on the opposite side of the ship to us and another one to get the alone human. And in that mean I would greatly appreciate you talking to me so I can learn about your Modern Dialect,"

Blake really didn't feel good about this but if he was stuck in this Pod was a good few hours then he might well try to make it interesting.

But there was no way in hell that Blake was going to reveal too much about the Empire and the state of the galaxy just in case this computer system was the reason why so many billions of humans were missing.

Blake seriously didn't want the rest of the Empire to suffer a similar fate, let alone sexy Nathan, Patrick and Ruby.

## CHAPTER 10

The entire Generation Ship was seriously starting to annoy Nathan now, it was just such a stupid design that it was like a maze with so many damn twists, turns and confusing little chambers that Nathan was extremely glad when he finally made it to what looked like an outside area.

Nathan went out of some glass doors that opened automatically and the outside was simply stunning. The green space was an immense wonderful circle filled with the richest, thickest, fluffiest green grass that Nathan had ever seen before.

The green space had to easily be a good five square kilometres that made it seem small compared to some of the chambers and rooms that Nathan had explored in the past three hours, but this had to be the most beautiful. It was even better that there were ten immense apple trees neatly scattered about the area providing a great amount of shade and texture and depth to something that might have looked a little dull without them.

Nathan looked up at the delightful stars and planets and it was great to see *The Curious* and The *Deliverance* were still there in one piece.

Nathan kept walking through the green space and the sound of running water was a nice surprise and it was great to see a little stream running through the area.

It must have been delightful back in the day to have something like this, and Nathan had to admit he had never seen anything like it. Having access to such a garden was a rarity in the Empire and Nathan had been twenty-five before he saw grass for the first time.

It was all stunning and the billions of people on the Generation ship must have had so much fun playing, talking and maybe picnicking out here. Nathan just smiled at the very idea that these people could do those things so easily when it was so much harder for modern-day Empire citizens to do the same.

Nathan came out walking through the green space until he noticed the ruins of something made from white marble. He went over to it and realised he had seen something like this before.

He would have recognised the white marble raised platform, six marble pillars and the marble table anywhere. This was similar to what Empire planets had that elected their Planetary Governor instead of it running in families.

This had to be some kind of platform where political debates would happen, votes would be held and business would be conducted.

Nathan would have loved to have his equipment with him so he could have tested the material to see when it became a ruin. It would be amazing to know if the Generation Ship always had a democracy like this that used open spaces to do political debates or where the political structured shifted into a monarchy or something with a parliament.

Nathan just grinned like a child at the very wonderful idea of discovering that. He went to open his mouth to tell someone about his idea but then he realised that he was alone.

He was always alone.

The realisation slammed into him as much as the cold silence did. Nathan was all alone on the Generation Ship, he still couldn't get a hold of the brother and sister-in-law he loved, and he was seriously missing beautiful Blake.

All Nathan wanted was someone to talk to, bounce ideas off and he really, really wanted to see Blake again. He wanted to see his stunning eyes, his smile and Nathan would have loved to see his fit body.

But he couldn't. Nathan had no idea if they were still even alive and that just killed him inside. Nathan had always loved his brother and Ruby so the very idea that something had happened to them was horrific. And even though he had only known Blake for a few weeks he still knew that Blake was an amazing guy that he only wanted to know even better.

Nathan just sunk to the floor his white lab coat and thin battle armour pressed and rubbing against his skin. And looked up at *The Curious* and *Deliverance*.

It was just so cruel of them floating there in the cold void of space and Nathan couldn't even contact them. He had tried repeatedly but it didn't work.

The Generation Ship was blocking all outside communication.

A loud humming sound echoed around Nathan making him stand up and a large white pod zoomed out of one of the buildings surrounding the space.

Nathan broke out into a fighting stance for some reason when the large pod stopped in front of him and a part of it dissolved. Revealing a very happy smiling and beautiful Blake.

"You want a lift?" Blake asked grinning.

Nathan just laughed. Blade had clearly been busy and he waved at Ruby and Patrick as they were inside the... whatever this pod was and now that they were together again Nathan just knew they would find out the secrets of the ship.

Because together the four of them were unstoppable.

## CHAPTER 11

Blake was so relieved to have beautiful, sexy Nathan back with him and at least the man he was falling more and more for was okay. Blake had checked Nathan's back like he had wanted to and that came with the added bonus of seeing how hot and fit Nathan's body was. Thankfully his back was only bruised and it looked like it was starting to heal anyway.

All of them were packed tightly into the self-driving car that Blake had taught a ton about the modern language and thankfully the computer had been somewhat useful. It had managed to tell him a few dates about when things had started to go wrong but the computer didn't know about the ship or anything.

And the dates the computer had given Blake were in Old Calendar that Blake had no idea how to translate into the Modern Calendar so he had no idea if things had started to go wrong according to the computer yesterday, a century ago or ten thousand years ago.

There was simply no way to know without getting access to the Command Bridge which sadly the computer didn't know what that was but the computer had agreed to take them to the Driving Seat.

Blake was so glad he had Ruby, Patrick and sexy Nathan with him. He didn't think he could do this without them.

"We know how the Generation Ship fed its people, formed a government and fertilised the plants," Nathan said.

"And bro, we know how they cared for the injured too. Me and Ruby found ourselves in a rough medical wing with beds, cell regeneration and bone-fixers,"

Blake bit his lip and was glad to see Nathan had the same reaction. He hated to imagine how primitive and painful those medical devices were.

"And we also found," Ruby said, "that the Generation Ship had three main cultures. That were defined by class and trades and even marriage,"

Blake leant closer to them because that was fascinating.

"We found pictures, art and sculptures depicting really rich people in the clothes of government officials, maybe royalty and other rich people," Ruby said.

Blake nodded. It seemed that humanity could

never get the need for greed and power and influence out of its system.

"Then we found references to workers and other classes of people that were seem as, not quite inferiors, but people less fortunate them the people in robes," Ruby said.

Blake was more impressed with the culture of the Generation ship. The vast majority of the Empire didn't really have classes anymore besides from the Government class and the working class always lived very comfortably. But it was impressive to see a culture so open and non-judgemental towards people of a so-called lower station.

Then Blake noticed how Patrick and Ruby weren't talking anymore and they were simply looking at the floor.

"What's wrong?" Nathan asked.

"Bro, there ain't a good way to explain this but we found entire rooms dedicated to the Emperor,"

The revelation just hit Blake in the chest. He had no idea what that meant or how that was even possible.

"Is it our Emperor?" Nathan asked.

"Bro of course it is. The paintings were the exact same as our ones. The references, tones and syntax were all identical. How the hell did people three hundred thousand years ago before the Emperor had revealed himself knew about him?"

And that was the question. Blake had read many historical reports from the Inquisition, that scary top-secret organisation that acted as the Empire's ultimate security service, that proposed the Emperor was easily three million years old.

"It's possible but it makes no sense. Why would the Emperor send people away that could have helped him when the time came to reveal himself and claim humanity as his own?" Blake asked.

"No clue mate,"

Blake looked at Nathan and as beautiful as he was he didn't look like he had an idea either.

"What about the third class?" Blake asked.

Patrick grinned. "That's were things get even more interesting. It turns out there was a class of people dedicated to researching the Emperor's armour in the ship,"

Blake's eyes just widened. How the hell could these people have access to something that belonged to the Emperor himself? And even if they did have something like that how the hell did an entire class of people rise out of that situation?

"I really hope the Driving Seat can tell us more," Blake said.

Nathan just laughed and hugged him. Blake really loved Nathan's warm and gentle and wonderful touch against his.

But the silence between them all spoke volumes. They were all getting more and more fearful about the Generation Ship and its implications on the Empire could be staggering.

And as Blake knew from history when a

civilisation was shaken to its very core. It always ended badly and spelled the end for a civilisation.

# THE LOST GENERATION

# CHAPTER 12

Nathan was just amazed as he stepped out of the white pod or "car" as it was apparently called and into the Driving Seat. It was a strange little design but it was beautiful. The entire chamber was a spherical design with golden walls that were perfectly smooth, there were immense floor-to-ceiling windows that allowed them to overlook the entire Generation Ship and there was a single grey throne in the middle.

Nathan realised that they were on top of the spires of the ship and this was probably where the ship had glowed earlier.

The air was perfectly warm and scented with apples, grapes and wine. It was a heavenly smell that Nathan never wanted to leave from but considering this was where the Generation Ship was piloted from it was strange how there was only one command throne.

"Who wants to sit down?" Ruby asked grinning.

Nathan really didn't want any of them sitting

down on the command throne until they at least understood a little about how the ship worked. The last thing Nathan wanted to do was sit on the throne and learnt that they needed a special implant to harass the raw power of the ship.

At least they were the sort of accidents that alien historical records showed could happen in other cultures so why not humans?

"There are no holograms, computers or anything bro,"

Nathan just shrugged. For a generation ship he was expecting a hell of a lot more from the Driving Seat. He was expecting some kind of navigation equipment, computers or just something for a crew to use but there wasn't any.

The car hummed to life before dissolving away like it had never been there at all. Nathan bit his lip because now they were trapped.

"Did anyone's equipment survive?" Nathan asked.

Everyone shook their heads.

"Why would the Generation Ship strip us of modern equipment but not our enviro-suits that contain microscopic but more advance technology than what it stripped us of?" Nathan asked.

"The ship wanted to learn," Blake said and he was hot when he was clever.

Nathan nodded. "Of course. It stripped us of things like communicators, bags and other equipment that it already made. But I doubted Generation Ships had access to enviro-suits like ours,"

Then the realisation sunk in and it terrified Nathan.

"Are we agreeing that the Generation Ship is clever enough to make sure everything works, get rid of billions of people without a trace and it's smart enough to figure out what equipment to strip us of and what to keep?" Nathan asked.

Everyone gasped.

"What the fuck is this place?" Blake asked.

Nathan just looked at the command throne and went over to it. He gently ran is fingers over the smooth cold metal and it sparkled a little at his touch almost like it was willing and alluring him to sit down.

"I have to take the risk," Nathan said.

"Na bro-"

Nathan sat down before anyone could stop him.

Nathan hissed as he felt something pierce the back of his neck and something crawl up into his brain and then he couldn't see Patrick, Ruby or sexy Blake anymore. It was like they were distant memories of long-dead people.

He tried to look around the Driving Seat but he was just taken back by the large orange holograms all around him and on the immense floor-to-ceiling windows.

Nathan was shocked that he had so much information in his head. He could see the entire Generation Ship, every room, every corridor, every system flowing through the ship.

It was simply too much information.

Red flashing warning lights echoed all around Nathan and the holograms flashed more and more.

"Disengage!" Nathan shouted.

Then he collapsed out of the command throne gasping for air. His vision went for a few moments and when he could see again he was more than glad to see Blade's wonderful eyes staring into his.

"There's no way one person controlled this Generation Ship. It's too much information," Nathan said.

"Did you see any other Driving Seats?" Blake asked.

Nathan forced himself up and went over to the windows and noticed that there were exactly three other spires on the ship.

"There could be a Driving Seat at the top of each Spire," Nathan said.

"That is correct," a voice said in Nathan's head.

"What?" Nathan asked.

"What's wrong?" Blake asked and Nathan had no idea what to tell him.

"There's a voice in my head. It must have been implanted by the command throne,"

"That is correct and I must admit Captain you are acting very out of character. Didn't your training cover this implant,"

Nathan was about to argue with the voice but he knew that wouldn't do him any good.

"Captain, I am not detecting three other Captains

at their stations. As the Captain Prima you should report them for that crime,"

Nathan started to understand the Ship a lot better now. It was becoming clear that the Generation Ship didn't need a crew because everything ran off the brain power of four Captains sitting in four Driving Seats.

"Computer," Nathan said. "Please summon three cars for my fellow Captains and take them to their respected Driving Seats,"

"Affirmative Captain. I will make sure the Captain Betas get to their posts on time,"

"Thank you," Nathan said as he really hoped this was a good idea and this would bring them one step closer to finally getting the answers they've been hunting for weeks.

Blake came over to Nathan and grinned like a little schoolboy, he was so cute when he did that. "If I'm your beta does that make you my Alpha?"

Nathan grinned. "Maybe. We haven't shown ourselves to each other yet,"

"Emphasise on *yet* my dominant Captain," Blake said.

Nathan simply bit his lip because it was great to know that Blake was thinking about him in the exact same ways. And now they had subtly spoken about adult things Nathan was rather excited about it.

In fact he was excited about this mission Captain business a lot more than he ever wanted to admit.

## CHAPTER 13

As Blake sat down on the perfectly warm metal command throne in one of the other Driving Seats of the Ship, he really wasn't sure about this plan at all. Of course sexy Nathan was probably right about them all having to connect to the Ship to help distribute the sheer amount of information but he still felt uncomfortable about the entire idea.

This could go so many different ways that it was simply too dangerous but he still sat down. None of it was logical yet Blake also knew that it was the only way forward and his own historical curiosity was boiling over.

He just had to find out what the hell was going on.

Blake sat back in the command throne and simply allowed the throne to take him. At first it was nothing more than a pin-prick in the back of the neck and then a strange sensation of something crawling up his neck and into his brain but then he felt comfortable.

A few moments later the entire Driving Seat chamber fell away from him and the immense choking smell of burnt oil, rubber and cables filled the air. Blake didn't know what it was until he realised it was an illusion as it disappeared.

Blake's sight became filled with data streams, flashes of images and so much information filled his head. Blake couldn't believe he could see every single corridor, room and system on the entire Ship.

Then the pressure only eased as Blake felt the presence of three other people in the system too. Sort of like how people feel when they know there are people behind them without them having to turn around.

It was such a strange feeling but Blake was also really glad about it. At least he wasn't alone.

"What's happening mate?" Patrick asked.

Blake shook his head as he tried to make all the flashing images come together for a moment and he simply willed it and there were clear images for him to see, study and enjoy.

"Just will the information to come together and it will," Blake said.

"Wow mate. That's sick," Patrick said. And Blake had to agree it was great to see all the information come together.

"You four are not Generation Ship material. You four are interlopes," a computerised voice said in Blake's mind.

"We serve the Emperor," Blake said hoping that would make the voice calm down.

"The Emperor? It is impossible for him to be alive. We killed him. We savaged his corpse and sacrificed him to the King's health," the computer said. "It is impossible. Prepare to be destroyed interlopers,"

"Computer disengagement protocols. Captain Prima clearance," Nathan said.

Blake hissed a little as he felt a tiny amount of heat built up in his brain and then it went back to normal as presumably the implant that the ship did was melted away.

"How did you know that would work?" Blake asked.

"I didn't. I just guessed that if the Emperor was involved then he wouldn't have been stupid enough to create a system without a way to destroy it," Nathan said.

Blake completely agreed. The last thing he ever would have said or called the Emperor, was stupid.

"I've found something strange," Ruby said. "I cannot find any security footage, information or data from a one-week time period and after that the records show no humans were ever found on board again,"

Blake gasped. This was the information they had been looking for but it was just annoying as hell that it was missing.

"Data recovery required. Captain Prima

Clearance," Nathan said but nothing happened so clearly the data was well and truly lost.

"Bro you thinking about this wrong. In all cultures there are signs of their downfall way before it actually falls. This culture ain't gonna be any different,"

Blake nodded and willed the information of the Ship to zoom out and he did what he did best. He focused on finding the first event that signalled massive problems for the cultures. Normal people never recognised these events as impossible but Blake had loved studying so many dead alien cultures during his undergraduate and Masters that finding these events were second nature to him.

"Here," Blake said bringing up historical records of a massive political fight that happened three years before the missing week of data.

Blake didn't care to read it to them because the Ship was already downloading it into their brains but it was a political battle about a group of rich people wanting to make the "Emperor Seekers" the ruling class of the Generation Ship and the Working Class and the Royal Class said no firmly.

Then it seemed these rich people inspired a mini-rebellion against the King and Queen of the time in an effort to make the Emperor Seekers the rulers of the Generation Ship.

Unfortunately the Ship said the rest of the files were deleted and too corrupted to examine.

"Do we think the Emperor Seekers are a cult or

something?" Ruby asked.

"Maybe," Blake said. "Nat can you see if you can locate this *Emperor Armour* that Ruby found mention of earlier?"

"Sure," he said. "Nothing. All information seems to be destroyed and even I cannot access it,"

Blake couldn't believe that and it seemed stupid in hindsight for an ancient culture to destroy texts, references and any mention of a major threat to their civilisation but this was only history repeating itself. All cultures burnt important things in their dying days.

"Wait bro. Can anyone access the lowest level of the Generation Ship?"

Blake willed the information to show him the entire lowest level of the Ship but nothing came up. It was like the information around him was acknowledging there was a lowest level but not daring to tell him what was down there.

"It cannot be any engines, shields or technology because that's all accounted for in the levels above it," Ruby said.

"So if I was living on a Generation Ship and I didn't want people finding what I was doing," Blake said, "then I would probably head to the lowest level. But who and what were they up to?"

"I'll send *cars* to your locations and we'll meet at the point just above the lowest level," Nathan said. "And guys, is it me or does anyone feel like they're being watched?"

Blake disconnected with everyone else and now he was back in the real-world he actually agreed. He couldn't help but feel like even now something or someone was watching him in the shadows.

Blake had to get to the lowest level now.

# CHAPTER 14

Nathan was so glad to see the amazing man he loved step out of the strange white pod as Patrick, Ruby and perfect Blake joined him in a long sterile white corridor with a holographic lift leading down to the lowest level.

The corridor itself felt so strange and isolated when Nathan was standing here alone but he could have sworn that he could see a figure standing behind him out of the corner of his eye. It was so fascinating and just annoying at the same time because it felt like each step closer Nathan took to get to the truth he was only opening more and more doors leading to more questions.

But this was why he absolutely loved his amazing job and it was even better he got to do it with the family and man he loved.

"I tried to get the car computer to tell me about the Emperor Seekers on the way over but they didn't know anything," Blake said.

Nathan wasn't surprised. He had tried the same but his computer had glitched several times on the way over here and he had even sworn he saw a figure's image flash up on a hologram.

Nathan shook his head. Maybe he just needed some sleep, drink and a nice hot meal. The past few hours had hardly been stress-free.

Patrick went over to the holographic lift and he stepped inside, Ruby joined him and then Nathan grabbed Blake's hand and they both followed.

"Why are you holding my hand?" Blake asked like a little teenage boy.

"Because whatever we face down here I've got you," Nathan said more to himself than anything else.

The holographic lift took them down a long metal tunnel in the pitch darkness and then the smell of rust, damp and mould filled the air for a few moments until the hum of enviro-systems flared to life removing the smell completely.

"Why didn't the systems work down here unlike the rest of the ship?" Nathan asked. There had to be a reason.

"Welcome Home Captain Prima," a computerised voice said.

Nathan felt the lift stopped and the bright white lights flickered on and Nathan gasped in utter horror.

Nathan had seen so many weird things in his time but he had never ever seen a workshop like this. The large metal walls of the lowest level seemed to stretch on endlessly but the walls were covered in skin, teeth and photos of the Emperor.

There was even a brown painting of the Emperor that Nathan didn't even want to know what was used as paint. This entire lower level seemed to be dedicated to the worship, investigating and sacrifice to the Emperor.

Nathan went deeper into the lowest level with the others close behind him and he went over to some work benches. It was strange that the benches were made from wood like those of Old Earth. The benches were filled with images of the Emperor, warzones and damaged tanks.

None of this made any sense and then Ruby screamed a little and Nathan looked at her.

All of them went over to Ruby and Nathan gasped as he saw there was a skeleton made from plastic that was hammered out onto the floor with the largest nails Nathan had ever seen.

"Why?" Nathan asked. He just couldn't understand what this place was let alone what the hell this place meant to the ship. "And why was this the Captain's home,"

"I can answer that," Blake said.

Nathan was surprised that Blake was tens of metres away from them by now so they all went over to him and Nathan just shook his head when they saw the remains of military uniforms worn by a range of armies from Old Earth.

"The Captain had to live here at some point or another to have this particular military uniform here and, what's that?" Blake said going over to the uniform and moving a shirt off something.

Nathan gasped. The shirt had been covering solid gold armour, a chest plate to be precise, it was stunningly beautiful with diamonds, sapphires and blood embedded into the metal.

"Could that be... could that actually be armour worn by the Emperor himself?" Ruby asked.

Nathan shrugged. If it was then the four of them were going to be immensely wealthy and famous but it also didn't answer a simple question about the existence of this place. And when he had been connected to the Ship's system the second time he had seen the Captain's living quarters and they were all in the spires and not down here.

"We have to return to the Spires," Nathan said. "We need to learn exactly what the last Captains of this Ship were like and I for one would love to know some basic facts about this Ship,"

"Like what bro?"

"How many generations lived on this ship is probably one?" Blake asked.

Nathan nodded. That was his main concern because he had a feeling that the Emperor wasn't only extremely clever if he was behind this expedition so he probably would have given the Ship all sorts of information to help keep the first few generations true to their mission. But even the Emperor couldn't control a culture without him being here.

Nathan had read thousands of reports over his

life about cultures creating their own mythology, legends and versions of history over time. Hell most planets in the Empire did that.

This Generation Ship had to be no different and he had a feeling that was the key to understanding its downfall.

Maybe in the end the culture of the Generation Ship believed the Emperor to be a God or Goddess amongst them and someone tried to become that divine being for malicious purposes.

And in Nathan's experience that always ended badly. In this case it could have meant the extermination of an entire culture.

# CHAPTER 15

Blake couldn't believe how much he was loving his time with beautiful Nathan. He had loved spending so much time with him over the past few weeks and on the way back up to the Spires, Nathan had come up with so many great suggestions for what they needed to look for now in the computer system.

For the past three hours Blake, Nathan and the others had been swimming through the great and wonderful amounts of information that the Ship provided them with. It was almost magical and Blake was starting to enjoy being in the computer system.

Before it had been scary with all the information flashing past him but now it was great and he felt like he belonged here. That was a massive relief because Blake had hated the idea of them having to keep coming back to the computer systems.

Blake was just flat out amazed over the past few hours about all the information they had discovered about the Ship now that they understood how the

Ship worked. And how to get the Ship to show them the information they wanted.

Right now Blake was reading through the Captain Logs of the 20th and final Captain of the Ship.

The sheer number of Captains, generations and the historical events of each generation was so mind-bending that Blake was so glad that the others were with him. He really didn't know if he could understand everything without them.

Yet Blake had to admit that the final set of Captains were just strange people because it made no sense why they were Captains in the first place. For the first 19 sets of Captains they had all been plucked out of the best schools and universities on the Ship. And they were very intelligent, knew what they were doing and the Ship prospered under their command.

The last set of Captains never attended school let alone university.

Blake was surprised at that because it made no sense whatsoever. And since all the Captain logs were in audio format and not signed by hand in stark contrast to all the millions of other logs by the other Captains. Blake doubted that this last set could even write.

That made no sense because Blake knew for being involved in the Ship's computer systems that school was a legal requirement for the first thirty years of a human's life and there were entire floors dedicated to different years of schooling.

This Generation Ship took schooling extremely

seriously and in the early days parents were put to death if they denied their child an education.

Then there were the disappearances that the Captains stopped the police forces investigating. Over the last ten years of the Ship's life there were over two thousand people missing and each time the police tried to launch an investigation the Captains shut it down.

Blake flat out didn't understand this.

"I found their birth certificates," Nathan said. "The last four Captains were all brothers and sisters and they were never registered at birth. They were registered at twenty years old by their father. No mother was listed,"

Blake just shook his head. It was amazing that on such a high-tech Generation Ship that seemed to track everyone's movements so perfectly and stored the records in extremely safe places, and yet it couldn't detect four births.

"Who was the father?" Blake asked.

"A nobody,"

"That makes no sense bro. Captains descended from the ruling class half of the time and then the other half the Captains came from the working class without any signs of hate for whoever was in charge. No one discriminated on class it seems,"

Blake was glad about that but it made no sense about how the children of a nobody that lacked an education became the rulers of the Generation Ship.

"Oh Throne," Ruby said.

"What?" Blake asked.

"I just checked what the 19th Set of Captains died from. They were assassinated at point-blank range. No one ever did find the killers and the records were marked as top-secret so only other Captains could see them,"

Blake just smiled. "There was a coup. The last Set of Captains killed the Set before them so they could take over,"

"Mate, it still doesn't explain what happened to all the billions of people and what the Emperor Seekers are and what the meaning of the chest plate is,"

Blake loved hearing Nathan laugh at his brother.

"I disagree. The Coup was probably done by the Emperor Seekers so they could finally take control,"

"That doesn't make sense bro. The political battle Blake pointed out happened three years before the civilisation fell-"

"But," Blake said, "you're forgetting that the last set of Captains probably did the Coup to get in place for the political battle. It was probably the Coup that led to the political battle seven years later,"

"I agree," Ruby said.

But Blake bit his lip as he just knew that Ruby was reading something else and as he swam through the information to see what she was reading Blake just grinned. She had discovered an interview transcript with the only known member of the Emperor Seekers that was ever arrested and tried for unknown crimes.

It was the man who claimed to be the Emperor and was later sacrificed to the King and Queen of the Ship.

Blake was amazed at what he was reading because the man truly believed he was the Emperor, the same Emperor who ran the Great Human Empire today. The man kept banging on about how he was the only person who could say the Ship from what was coming but he never explained what was coming to kill them all.

"Look at what the man said as he was beheaded," Ruby said.

Blake grinned. "He says. *When the Seekers hear about this. The Ship will die,*"

Blake just shook his head as everything was starting to become clear now because the Emperor Seekers had to be a religious cult and the man who claimed to be the Emperor had to be their leader.

And Blake actually knew exactly where the truth was and he had a little feeling that the Emperor Seekers were a lot more similar to the modern Empire than he actually wanted to believe.

Because he had a feeling that the man claiming to be the Emperor might actually have been him in one way or another.

Blake just needed to prove it to himself and the others.

# CHAPTER 16

Nathan really wasn't sure what Blake was talking about as he allowed the hot sexy man he was falling for to lead them all about into the lowest level of the Ship. The air was damp, mouldy and awful but right now Nathan really didn't care because he simply wanted to know the truth. And what the hell happened to this culture.

The culture of the Generation Ship seemed to be so advanced, modern and focused on education that it seemed almost impossible that these people believed in such lunacy as a religion aimed at the Emperor.

"I think the Emperor was far too clever for his own good," Blake said.

Nathan just folded his arms as he stood in the awful lowest level with the walls still covered in teeth, hair and other things that he seriously didn't want to think about but Blake took out a little knife that he had grabbed on the way down here and he grinned at them.

Nathan almost didn't want to know why he was grinning but it was almost infectious so he smiled too as Blake knelt down and stabbed at the floor.

"Has he gone mad?" Ruby asked.

Nathan shrugged and went over to Blake and he noticed that the floor of the lowest level wasn't made from a solid single sheet of steel or metal like the rest of the Ship. It was made up of small metal tiles.

After a few more moments of watching Blake try to lift up one of the tiles alone Nathan knelt down and held his hand over the floor.

"Open floor. Captain Prima Clearance," Nathan said knowing it wouldn't work.

Nathan was surprised when four metal tiles of the floor dissolved and turned to dust. Revealing what Nathan could only describe as a very, very early holographic computer connected with a bulky grey "hard drive" or whatever the people of Old Earth called them.

"You see," Blake said. "The Emperor wasn't stupid enough to let an expedition go off into the depth of space and not install a system that only he could access,"

Nathan nodded. That did sound like the Emperor and if he really was as old as some reports said then the Emperor had probably watched thousands upon thousands of human civilisations fall. So the Emperor had probably wanted this single civilisation to be spared of that fate.

Nathan looked at the hard drive a little more and bit his lip at the fairly fresh fingerprints on the only button. It was probably an on-switch and it was clear that someone had accessed it.

"Come over here you two," Blake said so all four of them knelt around the hard drive.

"Let's all press this together," Nathan said and everyone grinned like excited children as they all pressed the button as one.

Nothing happened.

Nathan was about to swear when the little hard drive buzzed, vibrated and sounded like it was about to take off. Then a very pixelated blue hologram of the Emperor himself appeared.

"I really hope that I have never had to use this you know and I don't know how my agents will hide this hard drive away but I know they will. I also know that humanity will fall here on Earth and as much as I try to fix humanity I cannot. Them and their damn politicians are turning this Earth to ash as I speak,"

Nathan was so amazed that he was getting to hear about what life was like on Old Earth before it fell.

"I managed to steer events here on Earth just enough so they would create a Generation Ship and we could get humans off Earth. Earth is most certainly doomed so I'm glad that humanity will not be completely wiped out,"

Nathan just grinned and hugged Blake. It was so great to know that the Emperor's mission had always been about ensuring humanity survived.

"I have installed this hard drive because I want to examine what happens and I want remote access to the-"

The hologram went dead and Nathan was so annoyed that he couldn't finish the message. He was learning so much and it was fascinating to hear from their leader three hundred thousand years ago.

Then a red hologram appeared. Nathan held Blake even tighter and he could feel Blake's excitement radiant off him.

"If this message is being played then the hard drive has detected something so criminally wrong that the Emperor has given up on the people of this Station. The hard drive has detected a full-blown religion and that the religion must have the support of the masses,"

Nathan just nodded. Everyone in the Empire knew how much the Emperor hated religion with a passion and it was why he made sure to exterminate all religious cults, countries and organisations when he united humanity.

And Nathan understood it from a historical point. It was amazing to see how many billions or trillions of lives had been lost to futile religious wars over human life and even more on human colony worlds. And then there was the fact that religion only bred hate, corruption and murder.

So it was fascinating to see how the Emperor had tried to save this Generation Ship from developing a religion because he had seen the damage it did before.

"If this message is being showed then the people of this Ship have abolished their democracy, monarchy and have fully embraced religion as their rulers,"

Nathan just nodded as the hologram ended because Blake just frowned at him as did Ruby and Patrick because they all knew exactly what had happened to this culture and it was just as heart-breaking as the rest of it.

If Nathan was a normal person living in the Empire then he might not have believed that over time the religious cult of the Emperor Seekers had worked their way into the top levels of Ship government, corrupted the masses of the Ship and turned them against their founding principles.

And just as history had showed repeatedly, there had to be people in the Ship that wanted to hang onto the beliefs, traditions and focus on democracy that had somehow survived twenty generations of the Ship.

So those people rose up against the religious rulers and the war and fight and killing burnt down the civilisation to the ground.

But Nathan still couldn't understand what had happened to all the bodies on the Ship? Why the Ship was still working perfectly? And most importantly who had erased the week of information and security footage.

It couldn't have been a human because there

were no more humans on the Ship when the security footage started recording again. Nathan just loved it that their work wasn't done yet.

All because it meant he could spend just a little more time with beautiful Nathan. And that excited him a lot more than he ever had the right to feel.

## CHAPTER 17

Blake loved the warm feeling of Nathan leaning against him and he had to admit that he was falling more and more for this beautiful man with each passing hour. It had been great how Nathan had convinced the others about his crazy idea about the Emperor and even though they had partly explained what the hell happened. Blake couldn't deny there were still questions that were annoying him.

And he hated being annoyed.

They all knelt around each other and Blake wrapped an arm around Nathan's wonderfully fit body and all stared at the hard drive with the sticky fingerprints of someone on it.

"I think we have to assume that some people found this hard drive," Blake said, "saw the message and took it as a sign that the Emperor was a divine being or something,"

Everyone nodded and Blake was relieved that he wasn't spinning crazy tales.

"Then I suppose that's how the Emperor Seekers got formed," Blake said. "There was an event that the people believed were divine in nature and then they created a religious cult dedicated to the being,"

"Just like in all the other thousands of cults from Old Earth," Ruby said.

"Exactly," Blake said. "But then if that's how the Emperor Seekers got formed, by misinterpreting a holographic message they were never meant to see, then why did everyone die?"

"Agreed mate. That's been bothering me too. If there was a war between the Emperor Seekers and the atheists of the Ship. Then why wasn't there a fraction that survived? And even if there was a fraction that survived for a while then they surely would have died because they couldn't run the Ship properly,"

"But all the systems are working perfectly," Ruby said.

Blake just nodded because everyone was making such perfectly logical points that it was just damn well infuriating how they couldn't figure out the mystery entirely.

Unless they were thinking about it wrong.

Blake smiled to himself for a moment before hugging beautiful Nathan tight and he stood up and paced around the lowest level they were in.

He was certain that this all had something to do with the Emperor's agents and what they would have done as they watched the Emperor's work burn down around them.

"What if we've had the answers the entire time?" Blake asked.

Everyone else stood up and Blake loved seeing Nathan smile in excitement.

"Earlier I wondered if the man claiming to be the Emperor actually was the Emperor in a fashion but by the time we got down here I had forgotten about it," Blake said.

Everyone folded their arms and Blake loved having their skepticism of him. It only made him work harder.

"But I believe he truly believed himself to be the Emperor and we know the Emperor had sent agents onboard from the beginning to install the hard drive. The Emperor wasn't known at this point. He was in hiding for hundreds of thousands of years before he revealed himself. He would only allow the people he trusted the most to become his agents for this mission,"

"Of course," Nathan said coming over to him.

"You've lost us bro,"

"I think the Emperor sent a handful of agents on the ship. They were his best friends and the people he trusted the most, but also would mean they carried about immense secrets with them," Nathan said.

"And come on, the Emperor has access to some of the most advance medical techniques humanity has ever seen. He would have made his agents biologically immortal as a thank you," Blake said.

Blake had loved that day at the library when he

discovered the Emperor used to do that to his best friends.

"Oh, Throne," Ruby said. "Do you… do you actually think one of them survived all this time?"

Blake nodded. "We've all mentioned that we feel like we're being watched. So show yourself!"

Blake honestly had no idea if it would work or not but he really hoped that this crazy idea was going to reveal something useful.

A loud shushing sound echoed all around them and Blake gasped when he saw on the far far side of the lowest level that a large section of metal wall was dissolving.

Blake just went over to Nathan and looked at him. "Want to finish this with me?"

Nathan laughed and grabbed Blake's hand and Blake almost blushed at the sheer electricity, chemistry and affection that flowed between them.

Blake led the other three towards the opened wall where he just knew that everything would be answered and things were going to get even more interesting.

## CHAPTER 18

Nathan was simply amazed as the four of them went into a small spherical chamber barely large enough to fit the four of them inside and the metal command throne in the middle. It was so warm in there that Nathan almost regretted wearing his white lab coat and thin battle armour under his enviro-suit.

The smell of smouldered pork, burning wood and burnt rubber filled the air, not so that it was unpleasant but it was just enough to make Nathan seriously want to know what the hell had happened here.

The walls were wonderfully smooth and warm to the touch. The ceiling was domed and tipped with a strange diamond-like coating but it was what was sitting in the command throne that interested Nathan the most.

Nathan grinned as he stared at the small metallic body of human male that had undergone so much cybernetic surgery that Nathan doubted that anything of the human remained. The brain and eyes might have survived but most of that was probably rotten now.

It was weird how a biologically immortal human would decide to convert themselves into a cybernetic monster for lack of a better term. But Nathan also understood that this man had probably not chosen to do it willingly.

Nathan had seen hundreds of humans that had undergone cybernetic surgery against their will and there was always the same cruelness of the workmanship.

Even this human's cybernetics were damaged, slightly twisted and the neck seemed damaged a lot more than the other parts of the body. That was normally from where the surgeons held the victim by the neck.

"I think we found the last agent," Ruby said.

Nathan nodded as him and sexy Blake knelt down next to the metal corpse and Nathan gently opened the metal eyelids.

Two very alive eyes stared back.

The metal chest started slowly coming up and down and the sound of light breathing echoed around the spherical chamber. Nathan was surprised he didn't jump but he was more curious about who the man was.

Blake started looking through the pockets of the metal corpse because there looked to be some kind of mostly destroyed jacket behind him.

"He's..." Blake said his eyes widening. "This is the son of Lord Commander Garrison, Third Lord of Europa and Sigil Of The Emperor,"

The words punched into Nathan's head like they were physical blows. Everyone in the history community of the Empire no matter how much they didn't know about Old Earth and the Unification War knew exactly who Lord Commander Garrison was.

He was the man who had singlehandedly beaten the Emperor in hand-to-hand combat when the Emperor had lost all faith in humanity after the Techno-barbarians had enslaved humanity.

This was the man who had convinced the Emperor to slowly reveal himself and start fighting his way across the wasteland of Earth and eventually he had conquered humanity and freed them all.

Without Lord Commander Garrison then it was perfectly possible the Great Human Empire would never have been created. And the Emperor would still be in exile.

And Nathan felt his stomach fill with butterflies at being in the presence of such a great person's son. Even the Son was legendary in the history books because he had been one of the few people who had tried to help the Emperor avert disaster and the Fall of Old Earth.

"No one else the Emperor trusted more for this mission," Nathan said. "And I doubt he had any help,"

Everyone else nodded. "I doubt the Emperor

knew many other people and if he did then the Emperor would have focused on preserving human knowledge before the Fall of Old Earth,"

"Wow," Blake said. "We're standing in the presence of the only person who survived the Generation Ship for 20 generations and ever since the Ship fell,"

The metal corpse's breathing turned deeper and more desperate. Nathan grabbed the corpse's hand and he realised that the corpse had been in low-power mode for so long that it couldn't function anymore.

Time must have eroded some wire, some circuitry or just something.

"You kept yourself alive for so long so you could see if your friend came," Nathan said.

The metal corpse gasped a little and Nathan moved so close that he could feel the corpse's cold metallic breath on his ear.

"Data saved memory. Tell Him I tried. Tell Him I saved what I could. Tell Him the Protocol was successful. Tell-"

Nathan just frowned when the corpse stopped talking and the smell of burnt rubber, wires and flesh filled his senses. Nathan knew that the corpse was well and truly dead now and also knew for sure that the cybernetics might not have been as unwilling as he thought.

But he just looked at the beautiful man he had really fallen for over the past few weeks.

"He saved some data in his memory banks

probably. Let's return to *The Curious* and *Deliverance* and see what he saved for us," Nathan said.

"Wouldn't miss it for the world," Blake said.

And Nathan so badly wanted to kiss him with them finally having the answers but there would be time for that.

But first Nathan just had to check that the defences that scrambled their last teleportation were well and truly off.

# CHAPTER 19

As Nathan stood on the wonderful, amazing square bridge of *The Curious* and transmitting a livestream straight to the bridge of the *Deliverance* as well, he couldn't believe how excited he was about what they were about to find.

Blake was still messing around with *The Curious*'s computer systems as he finished uploading the data from the metal corpse to their own systems so they could see what data was saved for them. And it gave Nathan a perfect chance to focus on Blake's rather wonderful ass, he liked it so much he had to pull his white lab coat tighter to hide his wayward parts.

The crew of the ship had certainly increased the temperature since they were away and Nathan was starting to sweat in his battle armour, but he still wasn't taking it off. The air smelt so much better than the air of the Generation Ship with refreshing hints of apple pies, vanilla ice cream and peanut butter cookies that smelt sensational.

Nathan was so looking forward to having one of them later on.

As there was a live feed to the *Deliverance*, Nathan just loved hearing the excited voices, buzzing energy and all the speculation about what they were going to find on the data. Some of the suggestions were crazy like proof of a conspiracy, proof of the Emperor's age and Nathan's personal favourite proof that the Generation Ship wasn't from Old Earth at all.

All three of those suggestions were great but Nathan just knew they were very, very wrong.

"You wanna mug bro?"

Nathan hugged his brother and Ruby as they both came back into the bridge with piping hot mugs of coffee for all of them. Nathan wrapped his hands around his and he was so excited when Blake stood up and nodded that the data was about to start playing.

"Let the truth be revealed," Nathan said quietly.

He wasn't sure what to expect but it certainly hadn't been a very in-depth dive into the exact history of the entire Generation Ship. It was so detailed that it would thankfully take years to explore it all but this was some of the most amazing data Nathan had ever seen.

And the metal corpse had even been kind enough to include a summarised version for them all.

"Why can't all corpses be this considerate?" Ruby asked.

Nathan completely agreed.

As the data scrolled past them, Nathan was amazed that the Emperor's Agent had always lived in the heart of the Generation Ship ever since he had first gone onboard. He saw it as his personal mission to protect it all and protect the people inside of it.

And for the first two thousand years everyone had worked perfectly but at the tenth generation mark things had turned weird and the Agent had no idea why. So he investigated.

Nathan was amazed that he discovered when he returned to the lowest level of the Ship, five men and two women had discovered the hard drive he had installed and so the Emperor Seekers were born.

At first the Agent had just watched them but as they accidentally stumbled (quite literally) on the Emperor's chest plate that the Emperor had gifted the Agent as a thank you present for doing the mission. The Emperor Seekers had only grown in their religious devotion to the Emperor.

The Agent had tried to kill them all multiple times but he was a politician, not an assassin. And each time he failed, the more the cult believed (and others that joined because of it) that it was the God-Emperor saving their lives each and every time.

The Agent hated himself more and more and as he observed the Emperor Seekers wanting to gain power for themselves by getting their members into Captain positions and getting the monarchy destroyed. The Agent knew he had to act.

Originally (and Nathan had to admit this was

clever) he was going to reveal himself as the Emperor and it worked at first. But he changed his mind when he saw everyone was worshipping him in the Emperor Seekers class as they studied the chest plate and became an officially recognised class.

Nathan couldn't have begun to imagine how weird that must have felt.

Then the political battle 3 years before everything fell apart happened and the Agent was captured, and officially executed. When in reality the Emperor Seekers were so obsessed with him they ripped his body apart and remade it with metal.

Not knowing he was biologically immortal.

Nathan hugged Blake extra tight when the data showed them that the Agent's metal corpse was trapped into that spherical chamber for years and until they found him. But the Agent had managed to hack his way into the Computer Systems so he kept watching, learning and hating what the Generation Ship had become.

The Emperor Seekers had grown so powerful that the people had rejected democracy and their monarchy in exchange for their divine words.

Nathan leant forward as this was the part he was utterly fascinated by.

The Agent watched as a version of the Final Battle Of Old Earth played out with the autocratic forces of the Emperor Seekers battling and waging a full-on war with the so-called resistance that hated the Emperor Seekers.

Of course the Emperor Seekers won but the Agent had simply had enough and there were over five billion corpses on the Ship that the Agent knew he had to do something.

So he stopped the security footage recording and he activated a very special gift that the Emperor had given him.

Originally The Protocol had been designed to be reactivated if the prize of human suffering was deemed to be so great that the death of everyone would be better than allowing humans to live in the constant cycle of suffering, agony and death.

And even though the ruling members of Emperor Seekers weren't injured or suffering. He could see how badly the remaining two billion people were because they were being whipped, slashed and incited into performing acts that were not divine in the slightest.

The Agent activated The Protocol so the Ship simply sucked out all the air and allowed the people to simply fall asleep. Then nanobots were released to eat away the corpses so they would never be found and then the nanobots themselves would be lost over a matter of years.

Then the Agent simply kept his cold metal corpse in low power to make sure the Ship kept working perfectly, it was safe and that no space pirates damaged it just so the data he stored was always protected, and there was a small chance that the Emperor could see it one day.

And it was that sole hope of the Emperor seeing this information that kept the Agent alive through all the torment, torture and suffering he had gone through.

"Wow," Nathan said.

"Yeah. Just wow," everyone else said.

Nathan listened to the livestream from the *Deliverance* and he actually had to make sure it was still working and it was. Everyone on both ships and bridges were simply too stunned for words because it just went to show that as advanced as humanity got with all their space miles, technology and ships, humanity was always fragile no matter where they were.

But Nathan was so glad that the truth was finally out because it gave humanity a chance to learn from the past, improve their present and most importantly protect their future so what happened on the Generation Ship should never ever happen again.

And Nathan just hugged Blake even tighter because it was only because they had worked together that they had discovered the truth.

And Nathan was really interested in what else they might find if they kept working together and hopefully a lot, lot closer.

# CHAPTER 20

"The Emperor Protects,"

Blake just finished up with the Commander of the space sector and send his preliminary report back to Earth so hopefully researchers there could start to study this information in a lot more depth, and as much as Blake would have loved to do that himself he had new orders.

Blake seriously loved being back on the bridge of the *Deliverance* with its wonderful large floor-to-ceiling windows, its oval shape and its empty tiers upon tiers of holographic computers. It was so great to be alone in the place he loved as the command crew and Charlotte were out celebrating the end of another successful mission in the Emperor's name.

Blake had to admit he was looking forward to when the enviro-systems flushed the bridge with clean, refreshing air in the next few seconds because the crew's intense obsession with strong bitter coffee smelt amazing but it was a little too strong for Blake's senses at the moment.

Blake just stared out into the icy cold void of space and at the amazing blade-like ship of *The Curious* and he just felt terrible. It was only now that he had new orders to return to the Sector's Base to resupply and go out to explore more distress signals that he truly realised just how much he had loved these past few weeks or months.

His time with Nathan had been so wonderful, relaxing and fascinating that he really didn't want it to end at all. He wanted nothing more than to be with Nathan and be right at his side exploring the mysteries of the past, exploring wrecks and just being the amazing couple that he knew they could be.

But Nathan was probably too busy with this Generation Ship for a relationship. Blake had been there on the bridge of *The Curious* when Nathan had ordered a savage ship from the nearest Forge World to come and help Nathan take the Generation Ship somewhere they could study every single metal panel, screw and line of code inside the Ship.

Blake just smiled because doing that himself and being a part of it would be brilliant for him.

And Blake actually wasn't sure if he was upset or disappointed or angry at himself for giving up history after his doctorate. He wasn't because he was more than glad he had joined the Empire Army, but now he realised he was a historian and scientist through and through.

And besides from Nathan there was nothing

more that he loved.

Blake was about to contact *The Curious* in an effort to reach Nathan when there was a knock at the Bridge's large metal door that sounded no louder than a whisper.

Blake clapped his hands and the door opened and Nathan came towards him.

Blake's stomach filled with butterflies and both of them stood there grinning like two schoolboys who honestly didn't know what to do with themselves in front of the other.

Nathan looked so hot, sexy and beautiful in his white lab coat and his thin battle armour underneath it. He was just so stunningly beautiful that Blake really was sure that he never wanted to be apart from Nathan.

"I don't want to go back to my old life," Blake said. "I want to stay with you, Patrick and Ruby if you'll have me,"

Nathan took a few steps closer and grinned even more. "Actually, that's why I'm here. I wanted you to know that I have the option to request your transfer to my division. Your ship and crew can join of course but if they don't then you can join me anyway,"

Blake felt his mouth go dry. This was exactly what he wanted.

"And we get to continue exploring the Generation Ship together," Nathan said extending his hand.

Blake was about to take it when he bit his lip a

little. "One question first. Why do you always wear that battle armour?"

Nathan laughed. "It's my father's. He wasn't anyone special in the Empire Army and he died on a world I can't even pronounce but when I was younger he spent every single night telling me stories of history. He told me about adventures, origins and expeditions of famous historians and he even showed me some pieces he had found on worlds he had fought on,"

Blake just smiled because his father really did sound amazing.

"So when somehow the Empire Army returned my father's armour because apparently he had sacrificed himself to save someone extremely important. I made a promise to myself to always remember and act like my father,"

"Besides from liking women you mean,"

Nathan laughed. "Yeah. I like men through and through and I really like the man standing in front of me,"

Blake pretended to look around and they both laughed and Blake went straight over to Nathan and kissed him.

The kiss made Blake's eyes widen as he had never ever felt a kiss so passionate, powerful and a promise of what was to come. He had kissed plenty of men in his life but Blake had never felt a kiss this passionate and meaningful.

He couldn't deny that he had wanted this for so

long and it certainly was worth the wait. And Blake could sort of guess that tonight they would be doing a lot, lot more than kissing and that was perfectly fine by him.

Not only because they were staying together and Blake was more than glad about that, but it also meant that they could continue to explore history, ships and each other for centuries to come and if that wasn't a happy ending of a successful mission then Blake seriously didn't want to know what was.

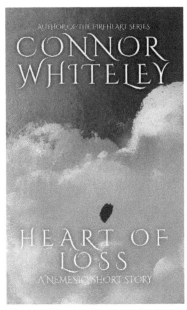

GET YOUR FREE AND EXCLUSIVE SHORT STORY NOW! LEARN ABOUT NEMESIO'S PAST!

https://www.subscribepage.com/fireheart

About the author:

Connor Whiteley is the author of over 60 books in the sci-fi fantasy, nonfiction psychology and books for writer's genre and he is a Human Branding Speaker and Consultant.

He is a passionate warhammer 40,000 reader, psychology student and author.

Who narrates his own audiobooks and he hosts The Psychology World Podcast.

All whilst studying Psychology at the University of Kent, England.

Also, he was a former Explorer Scout where he gave a speech to the Maltese President in August 2018 and he attended Prince Charles' 70th Birthday Party at Buckingham Palace in May 2018.

Plus, he is a self-confessed coffee lover!

Other books by Connor Whiteley:
Bettie English Private Eye Series
A Very Private Woman
The Russian Case
A Very Urgent Matter
A Case Most Personal
Trains, Scots and Private Eyes
The Federation Protects

Lord of War Origin Trilogy:
Not Scared Of The Dark
Madness
Burn Them All

The Fireheart Fantasy Series
Heart of Fire
Heart of Lies
Heart of Prophecy
Heart of Bones
Heart of Fate

City of Assassins (Urban Fantasy)
City of Death
City of Marytrs
City of Pleasure
City of Power

<u>Agents of The Emperor</u>
Return of The Ancient Ones
Vigilance
Angels of Fire
Kingmaker
The Eight
The Lost Generation
Hunt
Emperor's Council
Speaker of Treachery
Birth Of The Empire
Terraforma

<u>The Rising Augusta Fantasy Adventure Series</u>
Rise To Power
Rising Walls
Rising Force
Rising Realm

<u>Lord Of War Trilogy (Agents of The Emperor)</u>
Not Scared Of The Dark
Madness
Burn It All Down

<u>Gay Romance Novellas</u>
Breaking, Nursing, Repairing A Broken Heart
Jacob And Daniel
Fallen For A Lie
Spying And Weddings

The Garro Series- Fantasy/Sci-fi
GARRO: GALAXY'S END
GARRO: RISE OF THE ORDER
GARRO: END TIMES
GARRO: SHORT STORIES
GARRO: COLLECTION
GARRO: HERESY
GARRO: FAITHLESS
GARRO: DESTROYER OF WORLDS
GARRO: COLLECTIONS BOOK 4-6
GARRO: MISTRESS OF BLOOD
GARRO: BEACON OF HOPE
GARRO: END OF DAYS

Winter Series- Fantasy Trilogy Books
WINTER'S COMING
WINTER'S HUNT
WINTER'S REVENGE
WINTER'S DISSENSION

Miscellaneous:
RETURN
FREEDOM
SALVATION
Reflection of Mount Flame
The Masked One
The Great Deer

# OTHER SHORT STORIES BY CONNOR WHITELEY

<u>Mystery Short Story Collections</u>
Criminally Good Stories Volume 1: 20 Detective Mystery Short Stories
Criminally Good Stories Volume 2: 20 Private Investigator Short Stories
Criminally Good Stories Volume 3: 20 Crime Fiction Short Stories
Criminally Good Stories Volume 4: 20 Science Fiction and Fantasy Mystery Short Stories
Criminally Good Stories Volume 5: 20 Romantic Suspense Short Stories

<u>Mystery Short Stories:</u>
Protecting The Woman She Hated
Finding A Royal Friend
Our Woman In Paris
Corrupt Driving
A Prime Assassination
Jubilee Thief
Jubilee, Terror, Celebrations
Negative Jubilation
Ghostly Jubilation
Killing For Womenkind
A Snowy Death
Miracle Of Death
A Spy In Rome
The 12:30 To St Pancreas
A Country In Trouble

A Smokey Way To Go
A Spicy Way To GO
A Marketing Way To Go
A Missing Way To Go
A Showering Way To Go
Poison In The Candy Cane
Christmas Innocence
You Better Watch Out
Christmas Theft
Trouble In Christmas
Smell of The Lake
Problem In A Car
Theft, Past and Team
Embezzler In The Room
A Strange Way To Go
A Horrible Way To Go
Ann Awful Way To Go
An Old Way To Go
A Fishy Way To Go
A Pointy Way To Go
A High Way To Go
A Fiery Way To Go
A Glassy Way To Go
A Chocolatey Way To Go
Kendra Detective Mystery Collection Volume 1
Kendra Detective Mystery Collection Volume 2
Stealing A Chance At Freedom
Glassblowing and Death
Theft of Independence
Cookie Thief

Marble Thief
Book Thief
Art Thief
Mated At The Morgue
The Big Five Whoopee Moments
Stealing An Election
Mystery Short Story Collection Volume 1
Mystery Short Story Collection Volume 2
Criminal Performance
Candy Detectives
Key To Birth In The Past

Science Fiction Short Stories:
Temptation
Superhuman Autospy
Blood In The Redwater
All Is Dust
Vigil
Emperor Forgive Us
Their Brave New World
Gummy Bear Detective
The Candy Detective
What Candies Fear
The Blurred Image
Shattered Legions
The First Rememberer
Life of A Rememberer
System of Wonder
Lifesaver
Remarkable Way She Died

The Interrogation of Annabella Stormic
Blade of The Emperor
Arbiter's Truth
Computation of Battle
Old One's Wrath
Puppets and Masters
Ship of Plague
Interrogation
Edge of Failure
One Way Choice
Acceptable Losses
Balance of Power
Good Idea At The Time
Escape Plan
Escape In The Hesitation
Inspiration In Need
Singing Warriors
Knowledge is Power
Killer of Polluters
Climate of Death
The Family Mailing Affair
Defining Criminality
The Martian Affair
A Cheating Affair
The Little Café Affair
Mountain of Death
Prisoner's Fight
Claws of Death
Bitter Air
Honey Hunt

Blade On A Train
<u>Fantasy Short Stories:</u>
City of Snow
City of Light
City of Vengeance
Dragons, Goats and Kingdom
Smog The Pathetic Dragon
Don't Go In The Shed
The Tomato Saver
The Remarkable Way She Died
The Bloodied Rose
Asmodia's Wrath
Heart of A Killer
Emissary of Blood
Dragon Coins
Dragon Tea
Dragon Rider
Sacrifice of the Soul
Heart of The Flesheater
Heart of The Regent
Heart of The Standing
Feline of The Lost
Heart of The Story
City of Fire
Awaiting Death

All books in 'An Introductory Series':

Careers In Psychology

Psychology of Suicide

Dementia Psychology

Forensic Psychology of Terrorism And Hostage-Taking

Forensic Psychology of False Allegations

Year In Psychology

BIOLOGICAL PSYCHOLOGY 3$^{RD}$ EDITION

COGNITIVE PSYCHOLOGY THIRD EDITION

SOCIAL PSYCHOLOGY- 3$^{RD}$ EDITION

ABNORMAL PSYCHOLOGY 3$^{RD}$ EDITION

PSYCHOLOGY OF RELATIONSHIPS- 3$^{RD}$ EDITION

DEVELOPMENTAL PSYCHOLOGY 3$^{RD}$ EDITION

HEALTH PSYCHOLOGY

RESEARCH IN PSYCHOLOGY

A GUIDE TO MENTAL HEALTH AND TREATMENT AROUND THE WORLD- A GLOBAL LOOK AT DEPRESSION

FORENSIC PSYCHOLOGY

THE FORENSIC PSYCHOLOGY OF THEFT, BURGLARY AND OTHER CRIMES AGAINST PROPERTY

CRIMINAL PROFILING: A FORENSIC PSYCHOLOGY GUIDE TO FBI PROFILING AND GEOGRAPHICAL AND STATISTICAL PROFILING.

CLINICAL PSYCHOLOGY

Milton Keynes UK
Ingram Content Group UK Ltd.
UKHW020247010424
440366UK00013B/498